DUCK, DUCK, GOOSE!

(A COYOTE'S ON THE LOOSE!)

Karen Beaumont

Illustrated by

Jose Aruego and Ariane Dewey

HARPERCOLLINSPUBLISHERS

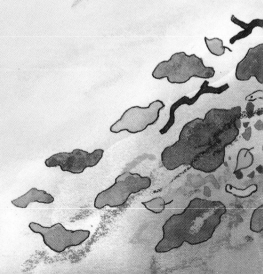

Duck, Duck, Goose! (A Coyote's on the Loose!)

Text copyright © 2004 by Karen Beaumont

Illustrations copyright © 2004 by Jose Aruego and Ariane Dewey

Manufactured in China by South China Printing Company Ltd.

All rights reserved.

www.harperchildrens.com

Library of Congress Cataloging-in-Publication Data is available.

ISBN 0-06-050802-7 — ISBN 0-06-050804-3 (lib. bdg.)

Typography by Al Cetta

4 5 6 7 8 9 10

❖

First Edition

For Steve, Challen, and Donelle, with love. —K.B.

For Juan —J.A. and A.D.

Duck, duck, goose . . .

A coyote's on the loose!

Goose, goose, pig . . .

And he's really, really big!

Pig, pig, pup . . .

He is going to eat us up!

Pup, pup, cow . . .

There he is behind the plow!

Cow, cow, goat . . .

Hurry! Run! He's by the boat!

Goat, goat, sheep . . .

Will we fit inside the Jeep?

There he is again! Let's go!

Sheep, sheep, mouse . . .

Can we make it to the house?

Mouse, mouse, chick . . .

Hurry, hurry! Quick, quick, quick!

Chick, chick, hen . . .

Past the barn and through the pen!

Hen, hen, cat . . .

Up the steps, onto the mat!

The window's open! Climb inside!

He's right behind us! Hurry! Hide!

Look! He's coming in! Oh, no!
There's nowhere else for us to go!

Wait! It's me! Why can't you see?
I just want you to play with me!

YIPPEE!